Simeon's Canticle

Mattie McClane

Myrtle Hedge Press

Contents

Simeon's Canticle	5
A Rebel Saint	11
A Visit to the Bishop	31
Clare's Parents	55
Mike Gibbs' Committee	63
Going to the Press	81
The Housekeeper Witnesses	91
Stir Fry Dinner	99
The Maples	107
The Bishop's News	117
About the Author	123

Simeon's Canticle

The springtime wind was chilly and blew tufts of Fr. Thomas' hair. Thomas was saying Mass as a favor to the neighboring parish's pastor. He entered the church with his walker. It was how the aging holy man got around these days.

He disliked taking it down the aisle and up to the altar but could see no other way to fulfill his duties. He hoped the churchgoers would be patient with him. Yet, when the procession began, Thomas felt as if his every step was counted, anticipated by the gatherers. There was no other way to see it; this Sunday's service was being led by an old priest.

He sang: "Through Him, with Him, and in Him in the unity of the Holy Spirit. God, Almighty Father. All glory and honor is yours, forever and ever." His voice crackled and seemed weak to him. He wasn't sure that the members noticed or cared. He believed they listened carefully to the liturgy, which was repeated at every Mass. He believed people would forgive his shortcomings.

He was not an actor or a celebrity. He was a visiting priest; the congregation was welcoming.

After the Mass, Fr. Thomas walked to the rectory, which was connected to the church. He waited for his driver to take him home. Fr. James had promised him that the members would take care of clean-up so that Bible classes could be held. Fr. Thomas was responsible for Mass only. He glanced out the window, watching for the white van. A man dressed in a gray suit approached him at the exit, extended his hand, and introduced himself.

"I understand you knew Clare Dall when you were a young man. I am with a group of clergy and laypeople who are interested in having her be made a saint. There's quite a campaign for her now. Can I make an appointment for my committee to talk with you about her? We want to know about her life before her conversion, when she was living in New York. That's what you can tell us."

"Sounds like you've figured it out," Fr. Thomas said. "There were other people who knew her then. She was very social. Why me?"

"We believe that you were in love with her," the questioner watched Fr. Thomas' eyes to see what they would reveal.

"I was not a priest then. Clare had yet to convert to the Catholic religion. Who else are you talking to if I can ask? We were young people who thought we could change the world."

"You know Jimmy Smith, Abbie Langhorn, and David Hurst?"

"Yes, yes," Thomas answered. They can help you. They knew her well. They were once her friends."

"They've passed on. Will you meet with us?

"Sorry to hear about Jimmy and all. So much time has gone by." Fr. Thomas pointed to his walker as if to show his own failing,

He lifted his gaze to the window and saw his ride pull to the curb. "Your name again?"

"Mike Gibbs," said the man.

"I am at St. Catherine's, the downtown rectory. You can call me there. We can talk. My driver is waiting," Gibbs assisted the elderly priest to the vehicle. Thomas was ambivalent now. He didn't know what he should tell and what he should hold back. Yet, he was certain that his memory was good. He could not forget a rather bold youth. How could he forget Clare Dall?

A Rebel Saint

Once back to his apartment, he unlocked a suitcase, where he kept important documents, including keepsakes. He removed three bundles of letters. He took off a rubber band that held a stack together. He settled into a club chair, then removed paper from an envelope. He studied her handwriting for a moment, noted that the cursive was small and unique. It was so distinct; it could not be mistaken as anybody's but Clare's. He read a few lines. She addressed him as Tommy, as only his mother had called him. Would he tell the whole story, about the intellectual crowd?

Then, everyone was earnest, with serious complaints about society, how some were poor, while others were rich. What had changed from their conversation? Now the Most Holy Father registered some of the same criticisms. Fr. Thomas recalled the young thinkers who were at odds with the status quo, who wanted to protest against management, the powers that held others down. There was hope with youth, but also a sense of sorrow; things weren't right.

Fr. Thomas recalled the meeting places, where ideas were fresh about 7:00 P.M. Someone would open a bottle of whiskey. The crowd grew loud, partly from alcohol and partly from political passion. Somebody always became excited, predicting police raids.

Simeon's Canticle

Of course, Clare was a bright one, well-read, and current with the events of the day. That is what he could love about her. She was a beauty who was plain, with a nose too straight. Her eyes sparkled like her intellect.

She had a mind that other people would follow, and Mike Gibbs was correct when he said he was enamored with her. He liked what she cared about, her advocacy for the have-nots, for people who were lonely and abandoned. She did not just care for people's lack of material goods.

The housekeeper entered the room. "You've had a busy day," Maggie said. "Mass at 9: 30 A.M. Did everything go well?"

Fr. Thomas smiled. He stretched his arm across the back of the chair, still holding the letter.

"Saying Mass reminds me that I am not so young," He laughed. "I'm glad to fill in as long as they will have me." He brought the letter to his lap. "A gentleman asked me about Clare Dall today, was interested that I knew her before she was baptized as a Catholic, says they want to make her a saint."

Maggie frowned. "The world must be short of candidates for sainthood. She was a rebel, wasn't she?"

Fr. Thomas agreed. "Yes, I suppose, yes. There were the wars. There were activists, folks against violence." Maggie only half listened to him; she was checking the trash level in the waste can.

"I'll empty the trash tomorrow," she said. "Have a good day, Father." She left abruptly, but quietly.

Fr. Thomas set the letters on his desk. He went to the refrigerator and retrieved a bottle of wine, nothing fancy. He thought what he would disclose to Mike Gibbs. When he talked about his relationship with Clare, he supposed that he was helping the Church, but also telling about his own youth.

He poured the wine into a glass. He felt knot-like skin on his cheekbone. It was a scar. He remembered the injury that came from a swung police baton at a pro-union rally. Fr. Thomas recounted how the fellow protesters nursed him. Clare summoned a doctor and then was compelled to answer many questions. The doctor was not sympathetic, he recalled the fallout.

"Doesn't a fellow have better things to do than to take to the streets?" the doctor asked.

He remembered the people gathered around him in the bed at a shoddy little house. He recalled that he didn't respond. He was an ardent follower of the movement. Some members went to jail, went on hunger strikes. At the time, his wound was a badge of honor. He had no remorse.

Fr. Thomas sipped his wine and returned to the letter he had been reading, Certainly, Clare influenced readers with her books, altered the mission of believers, changed the definition of social justice. The Church now lauded her writings and thought she was the spiritual impetus for a new focus on the poor. He knew her when she was an atheist. He knew her before he was ordained.

He could always see her backside at the typewriter. She faced the window with a view of clotheslines and fire stairs on buildings across the street. He walked behind her, putting his hands on her shoulders, massaging tense muscles.

"I wonder how effective we really are," she often mused. To the side of her was undelivered newsprint, the political leaflets that were to be handed out. They covered half the floor. She was surrounded by her words and the words of others, who hoped to make a difference when it came to social hierarchies and financial inequality.

Yes, she was a rebel, a secular one, then a sacred one. He knew exactly when she found the Catholic Church, but maybe that was the secret he should keep. There was a knock on the door.

Thomas opened the solid door, and it was Fr. James. He was always smiling, seemed happy with his vocation. He carried a casserole dish covered with crinkled foil. "My church women wanted to bring you dinner. They're good cooks; they drop off food for us regularly. They appreciated your saying Mass." Fr. James paused, handing the pan to Thomas. "We have a good parish."

"Thank you and them," Fr. Thomas said. "I'm glad you came. I need your advice. An organized group want to know about my time with Clare Dall. I knew her before her conversion and my becoming a priest. They say she's a candidate for sainthood."

Fr. James' smile disappeared; he became solemn. "So how can I help you, Thomas?" he asked.

"My inclination is to go to Bishop Mario. I've letters that might be of interest to the Church. I want to make sure this man named

Mike Gibbs actually represents a legitimate committee for sainthood."

"Go to the bishop," Fr. James said. "Dall is still so controversial, known for her politics. Most people think she was a Communist. It's interesting that you knew her well."

Fr. Thomas smiled, feeling the scar pull on his cheek. "Her story must be put in context to the times." He walked to the kitchen. He raised his voice, so his visitor could hear. "Many radicals then," he said. There were so many poor, destitute, and agitated folks. It's hard to imagine the desperation today."

Fr. Thomas faced his fellow priest. James smiled mildly, as if he were deferring to the older man's age. "Then there's the issue of mental illness. Wasn't she bi-polar?" James relayed his knowledge.

Thomas forcefully shook his head. "I'll call Bishop Mario. Her sanity has never been a question. Mother Teresa was also subject to criticism."

"She wasn't a Mother Teresa."

Both men knew the conversation had ended. There was an unstated impasse. James moved toward the door.

"I think it's chicken and rice," Fr. James said as he approached the apartment's exit. "It should be good."

"Thank you, James." Fr. Thomas surveyed the room, as if to see where he left off. He poured more wine.

The wine seemed like it made him emotional. He drank two full goblets and was glad that the church women brought him dinner. He was slightly bothered about his visit with Fr. James. Was he going to take up Clare Dall's part and defend her so personally? He was surprised about the passion he showed when talking about her. She had meant something to him in the past, but the priest counted how many years had passed since they had a relationship.

Yet, it was now a Church matter. When he advocated for Dall, did he unwittingly wish to absolve himself of a very turbulent period of youth?

Maybe that was not it at all. He recalled his physical strength when he was in his mid 20s. He was slender but muscular. For him, the years he spent with Clare Dall were a type of pinnacle, he was at the top of his game in ways. Their mission was spiritual, Godly. Only after he went to seminary did he realize how much that his secular friends were doing God's will.

He thought about Jimmy Smith, the best of his university class, searching, seeking for what was essential. He spent hours around a cheap table, discussing the laws before Congress. The humidity near the ocean made his thick blond hair curl; there was something magnificent about his observations of his contemporaries. He was looking for leadership, political leadership.

The daily newspapers spotlighted the arms race, war casualties, men who were in soup lines. Jimmy was not a single character, but a particular kind who came to the effort. Jimmy stayed for a few years; some were with us for only a short time; all were eager and engaged minds.

Jimmy went to jail for poor people, for their right to sleep in city parks. The city said their tents were unsightly. Jimmy argued with a city worker who came to pull out the tent's stakes.

The police were called: Jimmy was handcuffed and led away. He had one phone call and called the movement.

The money came from somewhere, and the movement was able to free him after two nights in jail. He was locked up with drunkards, drug addicts, and the mentally ill. Some hit their heads against the walls. It was an education that no college could give. Only the military might offer a more insightful experience. Tommy bailed out Jimmy. He was shaken up but returned to the house.

Jimmy's idealism was subdued for weeks: he was not so vocal at the table. Tommy thought that Jimmy needed to talk to Clare one-on-one. Tommy led Jimmy to Clare's office, where there were scattered books and bales of newsprint waiting to be delivered. Clare was on her knees, beside a couch praying. She said, "Help me God, for I am alone…"

Jimmy cringed; this was the celebrated Clare Dall? At that moment, Jimmy saw her as a phony, full of superstition. For Tommy, Clare's prayer was the beginning of his perceived calling. She was a superior intellect, and yet knew that her brightness was not enough. Tommy was confused and amazed. Jimmy dashed from the room as if he were horrified.

Tommy just stood there, waiting for her to say something.

She did. She said she had been reading the Bible, along with novels. "I've begun to see the work waiting for us. There so much to be done," she said.

"Tommy," she said. "I just think there has to be more, we're doing right things, but maybe it feels so empty on account of the fact that there's no one to thank. I want to, I'll thank God."

Her admission of faith brought the two together. Tommy and Clare took walks along the riverside, far from the refineries, on the green side of the city. They would often slip into a downtown church.

They were surrounded by Biblical stories, told in cut pieces of stained glass. They spent nearly an hour in silence every morning. In the afternoon, they drove the newsprint to the stands. After the evening meal, they parted; Clare worked on her first book most nights and occasionally joined the group for discussions. She wasn't a drinker then and put up with the high drama. She seldom talked about her blossoming interest in God.

Jimmy's reaction to her belief was so intense that she kept all things in her heart for a while. She was steadily moving toward Baptism in the Catholic Church. The publication of her *Study on Poverty* advanced her sense of God in the world and marked an interior change. She received the Sacrament on the very day her work hit the stores. Her secular friends wondered what it all meant for them and the movement. Some believed Clare Dall was a traitor.

For some, it was one thing to believe in God and another to join the Catholic Church. They asserted that the Church was the epitome of wealth and privilege. Some group members thought that the Church was mostly interested in enriching itself. How could she? At a party recognizing her book's publication, Clare Dall was confronted for her presumed hypocrisy.

"How could you write of the poor, then profess Catholicism?" Abbie Langhorn said.

Abbie was a Communist and thought Clare had both lost her mind and abandoned the principles of equality. She spoke forcefully against her former friend, suggesting that a new leader should take her place. A new leader could bring the group a resolve to fight unfair systems. Clare was now more alone than ever.

Clare sent copies of her book to Catholic bishops, believing that they, from their perches, could help the poor. With her book, she also sent a letter asking the bishops to open Urban Missions.

She imagined that these could be supported through whatever donations came in. She argued that the money would come. She pointed out that the saints knew money was not the primary factor.

Tommy was concerned that she had lost her following, but Claire predicted some would stay and others would come. She would start an Urban Mission, and there were always idealists who were up for a worthy cause. The cause was poverty, and she would not exclude any workers.

On the contrary, Clare was attracting attention from community leaders, from the connected members of society. Her book was selling, and if she would have been a different woman, she could have basked in her own glory. Instead, she put out two more substantial books within a few years. When praised for her literary achievements, she would give the glory to God

There was no perfect time to leave the Mission, so Tommy left for Seminary when the effort was stable, when it was more sacred than secular, and when Clare Dall was its director. It made him sad to leave.

Tommy and Clare had influenced each other; they had learned from the other. Now it was time to go. There were not extended goodbyes or tears; they both knew they'd be busy with their work.

Fr. Thomas folded the letter and returned it to its envelope. He stood, then carried his plate and silverware to the dishwasher. He leaned against the counter. It was so long ago but came back to him as if it were yesterday. There were still letters to go through. Tomorrow, he would call the bishop. He prayed for Clare's soul and all those people who were so alive in his memories.

A Visit to the Bishop

The church driver commented on the gardens on the way to Bishop Mario's home. Indeed, there were planters of tulips in bloom. There were azaleas, making a beautiful route to the clergyman's retreat. Was this the kind of privilege critics spoke of when they cited the Catholic Church? Fr. Thomas supposed that beauty was a perk to detractors. He knew Bishop Mario to be a typical figure in the hierarchy of the church. His residence was not particularly unusual.

The driver helped him remove his "metal legs." He helped Thomas through the wide double door. The carpet was deep blue, and the hall led directly to the Most Reverend's office. Mario greeted him as a friend. He grasped the tops of Thomas' shoulders, and seemed to fall into a quick embrace. "Good to see you. I don't make it to St. Catherine's as often as I should," the man said.

"It's Clare Dall who brings you here. I've heard her name often lately. It is true that the Pontiff considers her a remarkable woman. I don't know where that will lead. You say you knew her?

"Yes." Fr. Thomas sat down, put his walker to the side of the fabric chair. "I have some letters that might help the Church understand her better. I was contacted by a man named Mike Gibbs who heads a group calling for her canonization." Fr. Thomas sensed that he had the Bishop's full attention. The Bishop was a short, slender man. With his solid black hair, he looked younger than his years.

"Mr. Gibbs has been in contact with me as well. I assume you've taken sides regarding Dall. Are you corroborating her Holy nature?"

"Well, that's what I wanted to ask you. Is it appropriate, at this point, for me to do so? I knew her before and in the beginning of her ministry. Our spiritual journeys were parallel, meaning our aims became religious about the same time. If her early life was controversial, maybe too political, that is when I knew her best. We seriously thought we were going to rid the world of inequality," Fr. Thomas said. "I don't know that I can do her cause any favors or if I should try."

The Bishop moved to his desk and took the phone off the hook. "Everything about her life is being examined. You are taking on too much responsibility. If Clare Dall is to be a saint, God will allow it. Remember, it's God's choice here, not anything we do or don't wish for. Let's pray." The Bishop led Fr. Thomas in the Our Father, then sat down.

"Have you heard of a Dr. Tyler?" He's gone now, but they have his records. It seems that Dall's medical history is relevant. She was bi-polar."

"Yes, I know." Fr. Thomas adjusted himself in the chair and shook his head, as if to indicate that he was leery of the diagnosis. "I have letters from her that discuss a severe episode." He paused, wondered if he should go on. "Anyway, I have letters."

The Bishop sensed that Fr. Thomas was holding back but did not press on further. "Share what you know with Gibbs. If you think she was a saint, then speak for her. Thomas, I would pray that your memories are just and truthful, not the fancy of one who has a connection to a sacred celebrity."

Fr. Thomas appreciated the Bishop's words.

"I don't want to throw you out, but I have a lunch meeting," Bishop Mario said. "Don't worry, Thomas. I will talk to others. There is a meeting of the Catholic Bishops coming up. "He waved his hand. "I leave you now but will keep you in my prayers. God's will, remember that."

Fr. Thomas nodded. He was now left alone in the office. He situated his "legs" in front of him, and called his driver. He was encouraged that the Bishop was interested. The Bishop lent some credibility to Mike Gibbs and his group's efforts. He walked to the church van. Once inside, he instructed the driver to go to St. Catherine's sanctuary. He suddenly felt a great need to be in God's house.

Fr. Thomas sat in a pew beside a large stain glass window depicting the Presentation of Jesus at the Temple. The priest's attention was drawn to the picture of Simeon, the elderly man who recognized the child as the Savior. Fr. Thomas recalled his canticle:

Lord now you can let your servant go in peace/your word has been fulfilled/ my own eyes have seen the salvation/ which you have prepared in the sight of every people/ a light to reveal you to the nations/ and the glory of your people Israel/ Glory be to the Father, and to the Son/ and to the Holy Spirit,/ as it was in the beginning, is now/ and will be forever/Amen.

Thomas wondered what God was calling him to do. He was past his prime; his unreliable legs were a hindrance. He didn't feel very useful, and yet he felt God wanted him to tell the Church his memories. Still, what did he know about her life after her conversion? It seemed he was missing the most important part of Clare Dall's life. The Church praised her books without reservation.

He would read her texts, and he would try to become an expert on her life. Doubt plagued the priest. He was not as sharp as he used to be. He wondered whether he was now a match for 30- year old brilliance. Surely, Clare's words were meant for laypeople as well as the elite. Bishop Mario had told him not to worry. He sat in silence for a long while, until the church cleaning lady interrupted with her vacuum cleaner.

When he returned to his apartment, he checked his phone messages and read his mail. The Monsignor had sent him a letter about possibly moving to a home for retired priests. It seemed he wanted Fr. Thomas' flat for the Vicar. Fr. Thomas had not heard good things about the retirement community; he thought it was where the Diocese put its feeble clergymen.

Fr. Thomas decided to resist a move. He saw himself as suddenly necessary to Clare's fair assessment.

Some Church members would want to quash her sainthood. Some said she was too rebellious; others said she was mentally ill. Fr. Thomas believed in his heart her opponents' portrayal was a misrepresentation. He vowed not to be distracted. Her youth was the planted seed of her Holiness.

His apartment had a bay window and a view of St. Catherine's Church. He watched homeless men line up at the side door for goods from the church's food pantry. Each man seemed to have his own grocery cart. From a distance, it looked like a child's train with each cart seemingly linked together. Fr. Thomas saw the same men every day: the priest thought that the men had a daily route, going from church to church, then settled into the shelters at night.

He thought about hunger, and how people struggled to meet the most basic needs. Jesus loved the poor, but the priest doubted that the Savior intended so many to be without sustenance. The church could barely keep up with the demand for food.

He pulled the cork from a bottle of wine.

He went to his chair. He remembered Saturdays at the meeting house, how local grocers delivered less than fresh produce that was made into soups, Clare Dall cut potatoes, onions, and carrots for a big stew pot. A neighborhood bakery gave its aging bread. Meat was scarce but occasionally came in from a generous donor. On this day of the week, Clare and other volunteers fed the hungry. It was Clare's dream to serve the meal more than once a week.

Tommy felt useful on the weekend. He would lift the vegetable crates and carry them into the kitchen. He was strong and set out folding chairs beside a long rectangular table. He never tired then. After the simple supper, he would put them back into a spare bedroom that was used for storage. Their efforts were fulfilling; and they believed they were doing good for the common lot.

All kinds came to the weekend kitchen. Clare encountered some rough characters, but there was one who demanded her attention. She wasn't sure if he was drunk or just a trouble-maker. He took cooked carrots from the soup and mashed them with his teeth, showed them with an orange grin, as if to test Clare.

"If you are hungry, eat your meal," Clare advised him, not knowing what he would do next. He took a spoonful of soup, then spit it back into the bowl. Everyone at the table was watching Clare's reaction.

"I don't want my soup," the man growled. I want your soup," he told Clare.

Clare put her bowl in front of him, then went to the kitchen without saying a word.

The unruly man loudly slid his chair back and went out the door. Two bowls of soup steamed in the cold air.

Clare never knew who she would meet due to her hospitality. There were the poor, and the poor came with problems like addiction, illness, and criminal records. Clare Dall did not filter recipients of her charity. She ignored some antics and would often recess to a writing room. After writing, she would join, the thinkers, the idealists, for a discussion about their goals. He joined in.

The meeting house was never quiet, Fr. Thomas recalled. He listened for some noise in his apartment. He heard the refrigerator hum and some traffic in front of the church. Fr. Thomas wondered about the constant commotion of his early years. He then noticed it, but it did not seem to bother him.

He recalled the adjustment from the meeting house to Seminary. All sound was not the same. The meeting house rung with voices, chairs sliding against hardwood floors. There was always the sound of somebody moving, upstairs, downstairs; the sound of carrying boxes of print, a shuffling sound. There was the rattle of dishes, being put down and taken up. Glasses clinking.

Voices seemed muted at Seminary. The talk was low, considerate, even polite. Men said their prayers in a sober way. They had a quiet connection to the universe, creation, the earth, and old souls. There were musicians in the group; there were songs, the purposeful chants of even-keeled men. Some men were like Thomas, with bold, secular, past lives A few men battled with clinical depression. Some men's faith was nurtured in the home;

they had devout parents; they were altar attendants. Thomas did his best to fit into the new crowd, but he didn't like a sense of cloister.

He had been so actively involved in the world, and while he would occasionally go to different missions, he felt confined until his second year of Seminary. Then he received a letter from Clare at St. Benedict's Hospital. Tommy took some time off from studies and went to visit her. He was supposed to leave his prior life and concentrate of the Gospel. His time with Clare made him a Holy man.

Clare described her malady; she felt like she had been attacked by evil. She knew that Dr. Tyler had diagnosed the incident as mania. She stated she could feel "the hate" creeping up her arm. Clare had been writing a book about the hope for God's poor, and

Thomas knew she was an ardent activist for social justice. He believed that she has been assaulted because of her pure heart.

When he returned to school, Tommy asked about the prospect of there being a very real battle between good and evil in the modern world. Of course, he did not have to asked many holy men before a conclusion was affirmed. Indeed, God's people were fighting for the primacy of His Word: there was indeed evil that tried to cause folks to falter, to fail, to give up most Godly pursuits.

Tommy was then overwhelmed with spiritual courage. He not only had a calling, he had witnessed the importance of his vocation. Clare's testimony made him realize that Holy Orders were vows to take God's side, to stand with him at the foot of the Cross. He prayed for Dall, that she would be able to finish her book and go on with the Urban Missions.

Fr. Thomas surveyed his bookcase. He looked for Dall's books. He took down three titles. She had more that he was missing, He went to his computer and searched an online bookstore. He was surprised to see a book that's review told of her passionate and Biblical case against Russia and Marxism. The review said that Clare Dall could accept no state creed that was Godless. The book was her last, published only months before her death. The book was her final manifesto.

The priest inwardly sighed at her last venture into politics. Apparently, she felt compelled to publicly denounce the politics of her youth. Fr. Thomas ordered the book. He didn't know her as an old woman. She had once told him that equality was equality, and she had no beef with Marxists.

His thought train was broken when the phone rang. He answered it, huffing a bit.

"Hello, Mr. Gibbs. You've been on my mind. Actually, Clare Dall has been on my mind since we spoke," he said. He paused. "Yes, I'd love to meet with your committee. I've read through Dall's letters."

Mike Gibbs told the elderly priest that he had letters too, Tommy's letters to Clare. He would provide him with copies at the meeting; the meeting was set for 3:00 PM next Wednesday in the church's community room. Gibbs would also invite two other clergymen and a note-taker.

Fr. Thomas tried to recall what he had written to her. His memory was good, but much time had passed. He was anxious when the call ended. Bishop Mario's advice to remember that all outcomes were God's Will now calmed him.

~

Tommy loved Clare Dall. If she would have consented to a romantic relationship, he gladly would have agreed. The early group lived in close quarters, and the woman activist could have had many suitors. She was only interested in one man, David Hurst.

He was a weather scientist for the government; Tommy suspected that the FBI had a file on him for his vehement protest over the execution of Sacco and Vanzetti. Hurst often wore the same clothes for two or three days, a habit that lent him a slight odor.

Tommy thought Clare was in love with David Hurst. In the beginning, she made a point to see him. Her eyes twinkled with light; and her smile was brighter in his presence. They had radical politics in common; Hurst helped deliver the group's newspapers to the city merchants.

The couple was often seen together, but David Hurst was a no-nonsense type. When Clare took an interest in God, Hurst was concerned and told Clare to see "a mind doctor." He was interested in what could be seen, touched, physically known.

They stayed in the same small bedroom. After a time, the couple's disagreements became arguments, public and noisy. He would pout and brood. As if an act of betrayal, he sided with the ardent critics who could not tolerate a Catholic leader. David Hurst left Clare Dall almost immediately after he learned of her religious intentions.

Tommy consoled her, sat with her. Yet, when she converted to Catholicism, Clare did so with her whole heart. Her former friends were mean to her, snubbed her, degraded her, said she was brainwashed. She could only bear the mistreatment. She compared the abuse to the Cross, which was now real to her. It was hard to exaggerate the extent of her comrades' antipathy.

Her sense of loss over David Hurst was forgotten from her constant activity, and Tommy noted that Clare would never love anyone else with the same intensity as she felt for Hurst. She was done with Eros. She could not love Tommy as a woman loves a man. Tommy accepted this and was

Simeon's Canticle

contented with the friendship, seeing it grow as Clare expanded her contemplative life.

~

Within a few days, Dall's book rallying against Marxism was delivered; the book was titled, "The Failed Dream." Fr. Thomas began reading it shortly after removing it from its packing mailer. The priest wanted to understand Dall, her thinking, as an older woman.

As he read, Fr. Thomas discovered that she based her book on the Virgin Mary's revelations to the children of Fatima. Clare also believed that Russia should become a consecrated state. If it did not, the country would become a menace to the world, causing division, and disrupting peace.

Fr. Thomas realized that Clare Dall had the benefit of history. Marxism had not freed people but seemed to put its supporters in greater chains. While the philosophy's ultimate dream was to create a government where the common people ruled, Dall saw only the rise of dictators and tyrants.

The priest's gut feeling was right: he was convinced that Clare Dall would never deny the movement's members' goodness. She still believed in the power of secular good. She would have all people believe in Christ. Yet, her opinions of benevolent atheists were formed from experience: she knew most were sincere.

She was against state creeds not meritorious individuals.

The book affirmed Dall's respect for all people, even the people who criticized her.

The priest's eyes were tired from reading so much at one sitting. He marked his page and closed the book. He was happy that his friend's words were worth reading, even as she reached the close of her life.

The book jacket showed her picture. Fr. Thomas looked at the photo for a long time. The years had not dulled Clare's wonderful eyes; they still had a light that was extraordinary. If she wasn't a saint, the priest concluded that she was a rare human being, one who devoted her lifetime to unselfishness.

By the weekend, Fr. Thomas had read most of her work. There were a few books that he read as a Seminarian, so he reacquainted himself with those texts. The poor's plight was always on her mind. He wondered what childhood event or impression put her on such a lifelong highway.

Clare's Parents

On a hot summer day, Tommy accompanied Clare to see her parents in Scranton. They arrived at a small frame house in need of paint; the white paint was broken in places; its chips curled moving away from the wood siding. There was a chain-link fence, rusty in spots, enclosing the entire lot. It seemed to protect yard ornaments; there were concrete chickens, small statues.

Tommy and Clare had to open a gate: a sidewalk led to the front door. Clare's mother welcomed them with hugs and an open smile.

"I cooked your favorite food,' the mother said. She drew in a breath. "Can you smell it from here?"

"Oh Mama," Clare said, circling her mother, embracing her.

"This is my friend, Tommy Kelly. He's a good worker and helps us put out our paper." Clare also drew a long and dramatic breath.

"It's fried chicken," she said. "Thank you, Mama. I've missed you and Daddy so much. I told you I'd visit in the summertime. I did not lie."

The chattering group moved from the front porch to the dining room, which was in the center of the house. A large standing fan circulated the air and cooled the main rooms. The table was set, and the paper napkins fluttered a little from the breeze.

The mother went into the kitchen. She reentered, donning a floral apron. "Daddy just fixed the table, so you're just in time. One leg was wobbly," she said.

Simeon's Canticle

"I'm not done paying for it," she said with half a laugh.

She placed a huge platter of fried chicken in front of them. There were mashed potatoes, white milk gravy, and a bowl of steamed green beans. She called Clare's father. The family was seated for a fine meal.

Tommy took it all in. He was interested in Dall's parents. He learned that her father worked as a janitor at a lamp factory and her mother cleaned the houses of doctors, lawyers, even a judge.

When the plates were empty, Tommy helped carry the dishes to the sink. The family seemed so happy.

Clare had left home when she was 18. She worked in upscale department stores and took classes at a community college. Later she transferred to the state university but left after a year. She won a merit scholarship for high achievement, but college was costly; she was forced to leave. She continued her education on her own, seldom passing a bookstore with making a stop.

Clare was curious and seemed to have a need to go into society's nooks and crannies, delve into the stories of the downtrodden. Yet, she had never said that she was poor. Tommy realized that she never considered her family as being a part of unfortunate statistics that drove her daily.

Fr. Thomas put Clare's books in a stack on the floor. He needed to cook. He had been living on frozen dinners. Instead of reading his mail, he collected it in a pile. He was neglecting his own life and thought it was time to see what letters were waiting for his attention. He noted some appeals from the South American missions. He received so many solicitations from worthy causes.

An over-sized brochure about The Maples worried him. The retirement home was the furthest thing from his mind, and he did not want to move there while he had his mind. Why was the advertisement sent to him?

St. Catherine's pastor wanted his apartment for the Vicar. Would he be given a choice about where he lived? The priests at the home were physically and mentally disabled. Did the use of his walker make people think he was ready to join such a community?

He threw away the microwavable dinner tray. He put on his pajamas. He was scared; they might force him to go to the home. When he finally closed his eyes, he prayed to Clare's spirit.

A saint could help him, intercede for him. He needed healthy legs; the Church saw him as a burden. Then he corrected himself, praying to a friend! Maybe he was getting daffy, and they all knew it. He prayed that Jesus would remove his self-doubt, his negative thoughts, and give him clarity.

Thoughts of the future calmed him; he was prepared to meet with Mike Gibb's committee.

He wasn't certain about what he had written to Clare, but he was sure he could answer most questions about her. He had personal knowledge and what he had learned from Clare's books.

Fr. Thomas believed that he could clear up any misconceptions about her youth, her sanity, or political allegiances. He felt empowered and slept through the entire night. He had no dreams.

Mike Gibbs' Committee

The priest left his apartment about 2:45 p.m. He would take his time and walk to the community center. St. Catherine's grounds were beautiful; its many rosebushes were blooming. Thomas was optimistic, like a student who had studied for an exam. He felt like he knew the material.

The committee members were already seated at a conference table. There were wingchairs underneath the room's large windows. Mike Gibbs stood, as if to lead the priest to his seat.

There were three men who looked like fellow clergy, and a woman who sat at the table's end. There were thick binders in front of each man; the woman was busy with a laptop computer.

Fr. Thomas was surprised that they created a business-like atmosphere; they barely greeted him. One thumbed through papers. Another was reading. Mike Gibbs called for introductions.

Each clergy member said his name and home parish. The woman announced that she would be the recorder.

Fr. Thomas settled into his chair and waited for the group to begin. Mike Gibbs said he would be asking questions for the committee. He gave a brief history of the group. Their final report would be given to the Vatican. Mike Gibbs cleared his throat. "Let's get started," he said.

"We are most interested in Ms. Dall's youth, her 20s and 30s. The Church has documented her writings and her time as a Catholic activist. The committee has read your letters to her. They were given to us with the hope we could better understand a woman who led a conflicted life."

Gibbs placed copies of Tommy's letters in front of the priest. "I wish I would have had these before our meeting. I'd have had a better idea of where you're coming from," the elderly man said.

Gibbs put his finger to his lips, as if he were considering the priest's stated wish. "Do you know if Ms. Dall was a member of the Communist Party? You make many references to Communists."

"No, she wasn't a member of the Party." Fr. Thomas didn't like Mike Gibbs' tone. Immediately, he wondered if the committee was friendly and promoted his friend's best interests. "Clare worked with many people. She believed sincere Communists could do good works." Fr. Thomas worried that he said too much. He decided to give short answers until he no longer sensed hostility.

"Did she ever call herself a Communist?" Gibbs stroked a piece of paper with his hand, again and again.

"I don't know," Fr. Thomas said

"Let's go on," Gibbs, said. "In another letter, you tell Ms. Dall that you love her. Did you have an actual physical relationship with her? We don't mean to asked such personal questions, but it's important to establish if she was sexually as free as her other thinking. Was she a female libertine?"

"No, I was very close to Clare, and I did love her. We never had a romantic relationship. I did want one," Fr. Thomas

Simeon's Canticle

said. She loved only one man, David Hurst. I'm sure you know about him.

"You lived in a commune-like setting, young men and women living together in the same house, and you want us to believe that there was no sexual activity," one clergyman said. The others nodded their heads, as if to say the man had a good point.

"It was sisterly, brotherly. We cared about principles of equality; we were committed to equality," Fr. Thomas said.

"Everyone?" Another clergyman said.

"Yes, most everyone."

"There's David Hurst. He was Ms. Dall's lover. Are you saying there weren't more men?" Gibbs was growing impatient.

"No, there weren't." Fr. Thomas was beginning to enjoy shocking the conservative group. He wondered about their game. They certainly did not sound like people who wanted to make Dall a saint.

Mike Gibbs finally sat down. He picked up a piece of paper and waved it back and forth. "You recommended that Clare Dall have an exorcism when she was in St. Benedict's Hospital.

According to our records, she was suffering from mania then. You visited her at the hospital.

Which was it, a mental disorder or the devil?" Gibbs smiled, thinking he had left the elderly priest with no good answer. Gibbs felt certain he had trapped the man. "Don't you believe in psychiatry?"

"Clare Dall was sane, so I concluded that she was spiritually assaulted. Yes, I thought she could benefit from prayer."

"That is what you told her?"

"Yes."

"I stand by the opinion. Goodness is opposed in the world. "Just look at the Cross," Fr. Thomas concluded. He had enough. He stood, collected his letters, and walked out the door. Only when he was near the statue of The Sacred Heart of Jesus did he remember to go back and get his walker.

Fr. Thomas' heart leaped with joy. He was walking without his "metal legs" He went out and back in to the community center without assistance. Holy Scripture swirled in his head. "I say to you, stand up, take your mat and go to your home. And he stood up and immediately took up the mat and went out before all of them, so that they were all amazed and glorified God."

He went into the church's sanctuary, leaving his walker at the door. At the altar, the priest went down on his knees and thanked the Lord.

Fr. Thomas was afraid that he would awaken and find his glorious miracle to be an old man's unfulfilled wish.

He went to a front pew and studied the crucifix. He rubbed his legs; he stood; he sat; he stood again, testing his strength. The happening was real; he again praised God. He sat for a long time in silence. He felt Clare Dall's presence. She was with him today. The priest wondered what to do next.

For days, he marveled at his newly found freedom. He was now able to pace, feeling his legs with every step. He should announce the miracle to St. Catherine's staff, to Fr. James, and to Bishop Mario. He should tell Maggie and his driver. He thought that he should tell the world.

~

Fr. James visited, carrying the latest *Catholic Post*. He opened the newspaper and held a page in front of Fr. Thomas. The article's headline read: "Priest Says Clare Dall Needed Exorcism."

Fr. Thomas was at first speechless, then angry. Fr. James said the article was in print in five states and maybe more. His visitor said that it might even be a national news item. Fr. Thomas sat down.

"How did this happen?" Fr. James was aggravated.

"I met with Mike Gibbs' committee. The woman there must have been a reporter. The whole meeting was a sham."

"Did you say Dall was possessed?" Fr. James took the newspaper back. "Are you trying to take the Church back to the dark ages?" Fr. James did not wait for an answer. "The whole psychiatric profession will come down on the Church."

"James, watch this." Fr. Thomas stood and walked the length of the apartment and back, then again.

"I prayed to Clare Dall for healthy legs. I believe that Clare is a saint who interceded for me."

Fr. James looked interested. "That's wonderful, Thomas, but what does that have to do with the article?"

He looked at Thomas' walker, now situated in the corner of the room. "That is amazing," he said.

"Mike Gibb's committee members want to nip her cause in the bud. They were not for her." Fr. Thomas walked to the window. "It was clear to me that the group would use a bi-polar diagnosis or an affliction with demons to discount her."

"Do you believe that evil opposes good, that forces work in our lives?" Fr. Thomas asked his friend.

"Of course, Thomas. I believe that."

"Surely there are cases of bi-polar disorder, real cases, but other aspects afflicted Clare." Fr. Thomas searched James' eyes. "I am a witness. I saw the mania. I was there. She spoke in a man's voice, different accents. It was a powerful scene and one which I will never forget," he said.

"I see," said Fr. James.

"You'll have to answer to Bishop Mario, maybe the whole Catholic Church. I hesitate, but many find her an admirable woman: you're not the only one who thinks she was Holy," Fr. James asserted.

"Your testimony is heartening. God bless you, Thomas" Fr. James turned back to friend at the door. "I want to believe in saints as much as anyone." With that, the conversation ended.

Fr. Thomas put in a call to Bishop Mario. His assistant said the Bishop had taken a few days off; his nieces and nephews were visiting, Was there a message? Fr. Thomas was disappointed that he could not tell the Bishop Mario his urgent problem. He asked that the Bishop call as soon as possible.

He began receiving phone calls from reporters early the next morning. He didn't answer the inquiries; voice mail was working just fine. The calls were from national newspapers and a current events magazine. Fr. Thomas would not comment on the exorcism article. He sighed, wondering how the Mike Gibbs meeting went so wrong.

He had counted on privacy. Yet, he spoke what he believed to be true. He was not saying that mental illness did not exist or trying to misrepresent sick people. Fr. Thomas thought the time had come to see Clare Dall's entire life in religious terms. Saints were people who suffered as if it were part of their vocation. They were called to have extraordinary lives; lives that could only be spiritually understood. But now there was a real mess, and he had created it. What could he do?

He considered talking to the press. Did they need to know the whole story? He predicted that Clare's story could only become more sensational. He sensed that media outlets were out to sell a product: and cared more about the exciting tale than fairness or any claim to sacredness.

~

Tommy sat next to Clare who was at her typewriter. He watched her peck out the final words of the editorial.

"I think it's good," she told a small group of bystanders who wanted to witness the movement's fighting spirit.

A reader sent a letter-to the editor accusing the movement of being too idealistic, sentimental, and out-of-touch. The opinion infuriated the newspaper's volunteer staff. There was a feeling that staff members worked too hard to accept such criticism. Weren't they on top of the news, knew all too well what was going on in the world?

Clare Dall wrote the reply in the form of a column; it was fiery.

"We should run it on the front page," Clare said. She knew that that was an unconventional layout but wanted to answer the discounting reader with the movement's full force.

The piece told of miserable realities of poverty that were faced every day. There was a stench in the slums; there were diseased bodies, weeping sores, vermin, and lice. She asserted that the group was not too sentimental or unaware.

She rebuked the reader for not being idealistic enough, charging him with complacency. Poor people needed champions, because they were so often disconnected from the power sources.

"Would it be better to ignore the reader?" a staff member said.

Clare thought for a moment. She smiled. "I seldom think it's right to ignore important matters."

The column ran on the front page; and spurred more commentary: it started a dialogue about the movement member's beliefs, their goals.

The published editorial informed its readers, bringing the movement's members closer together. The editorial's placement in the paper encouraged everyone.

～

Fr. Thomas stood, walked to the pile of opened mail. He picked up the advertisement from The Maples. He re-played his phone's voice messages. He imagined Bishop Mario serving ice cream to his nieces and nephews.

He looked at the colorful brochure. He would act. Fr. Thomas began returning reporters' calls. He spent the afternoon giving long interviews. What did he have to lose?

Going to the Press

He told the story that he intended to tell Mike Gibbs. Gibbs' committee released an article that could only lead to misunderstanding. He felt obligated to recount the details of Clare's youth. He told reporters about the beginnings of her commitment to God; how she was dealt criticism for finding faith.

Fr. Thomas thought she might be faulted according to today's critics, but he reminded journalists that St. Paul, a main writer of the New Testament once persecuted Christians, killed them, had not one use for them. He was once more blameworthy than atheists.

His conversion like Dall's glorified Jesus Christ.

For the first time, he publicly declared his belief that Clare was a Holy saint, not just a well-intentioned do-gooder or an ardent political activist. He was the proof. He had used a walker, because his legs were unsteady and crippled. He prayed to Clare for healthy limbs, and she interceded, through her, through Jesus Christ, his gait was renewed.

He told the press that he realized his claim was fantastic, and he would not blame them if they questioned his account. Fr. Thomas invited the reporters to request his medical records; he asked them to see his now unused walker and watch him climb a flight of stairs. The elderly priest could do it.

He told them to talk to his driver who had assisted his daily travels for years. The driver no longer had to carry the walker for him, help him into the church van. Surely, his driver could testify.

He was asked about the exorcism article. He did not retract his firm opinion; true goodness is opposed by menacing spirits. He affirmed that he believed that evil battled with pure hearts. He cited Mother Teresa's life, the saints, their dark nights, dark years, earthly suffering, how they struggled.

Fr. Thomas spoke passionately and felt he was finally telling the truth, and the truth was being recorded and would be published. The reporters were interested, respectful, and courteous.

Fr. Thomas' words ran in larger, national publications; the articles were long and detailed, or they didn't run at all. He had inundated reporters with information and was pleased that the feature-like stories were positive.

The articles tended to put the young Clare Dall in with her robust times; they now had a historical perspective that could not be overlooked. If Clare Dall was a rebel, the era was rebellious.

Fr. Thomas had seen how opinion changed. In his heyday, Communism was a radical theory, but it was a hopeful philosophy to a nation of have-nots.

The despots were yet to rise to power, and no one had heard of Sen. Joseph McCarthy. The dew was still fresh on the pumpkin, and the ideology had its supporters.

The times shaped people; the times made Abraham Lincoln a great liberator; the Civil Rights movement made Martin Luther King Jr. a martyr.

Pervasive poverty made Clare Dall a Holy advocate for the poor. People could not be fairly judged if they were viewed in a vacuum.

The broadcast media came next; their signature vans parked in St. Catherine's lot. Monsignor Philip immediately took notice and seemed worried about the added attention. Would this be over before Sunday, when worshipers needed the parking spaces? The head pastor wondered if Bishop Mario was notified that a diocese priest was being spotlighted, in the limelight. Philip was angry.

Bishop Mario's call came quickly after Monsignor Philip's complaint. Fr. Thomas thought the Bishop was made aware of the media's presence. He was given a heads up. The Bishop asked to see Fr. Thomas.

Meanwhile, the cameras rolled; the priest again told the very detailed story for television.

~

Bishop Mario ushered Fr. Thomas to a chair. The Bishop moved around his office like a man who wanted to settle in for a discussion. He adjusted the blinds, fending off the afternoon sun.

He sat down, rolling his chair so that it faced the visiting priest. He turned and took the phone off the hook.

"Tell me Thomas, what's going on?" He did not wait for a reply. "You know, the Diocese has a communication staff, folks whose job it is to deal with the media. "You should have followed the right channels. I'm getting phone calls from all over, wanting to know what is happening here."

Simeon's Canticle

"I can't honestly answer them, because you've kept me in the dark. Apparently, you are making a very public case for Dall's sainthood. I feel like you're going rogue on the Church. Am I right?"

"I called you first, but you were busy with family. The meeting with the Gibbs fellow did not go well. The committee was not interested in my story. Gibbs was misrepresenting Clare Dall and seemed only interested in putting her in a bad light. He misrepresented himself to me; he was not for her."

The Bishop turned back to his phone, picking us the receiver from the desk, He dialed a short number. "Would you come to my office?" he said. Then he set the receiver down on his desk.

"So, let me understand. "You've become Clare Dall's advocate? You're telling the media that she was a saint? The Bishop looked to him, wanting an answer this time.

"Yes," Fr Thomas said. "Gibbs released an unfair and negative account of our meeting to the press first. When I agreed to the committee's meeting, I thought there would be a degree of privacy. My understanding was that I was sharing information with the Church. I responded to leaked information, thinking it was better to share the whole story rather than a misleading half."

A man appeared at the office's doorway. "Come in," the Bishop said. "Thomas, this is Joey Cree, the Diocese's communication officer. Joey, this is Fr. Thomas, the priest who has been the topic of recent inquiries."

The introductions interrupted Thomas. The priest smiled at the man, went silent.

"Thomas, are you satisfied now? Can you let it go?" The Bishop awaited his answer, thinking he would assent.

"I'd like to address the Conference of Bishops. I've gone this far." He paused. "I'd like to tell the Church."

Bishop Mario looked at Joey, then Thomas. "The Conference is for business. It's for important business."

"Most Reverend, my legs are healed."

The Bishop had heard the story, and doubted it was a true miracle. "There is a such thing as remission."

Thomas shook his head. "Please allow me to tell the story to the Bishops. I ask this in Christ's name."

Bishop Mario wasn't sure how to finish with Fr. Thomas' insistence that a story needed to be told.

"Can you give me a few minutes before the clergy?" Thomas said.

"I don't set the agenda for the meeting, he said. The Bishop was convinced that the old man's persistence was not going away.

"You can go," he told his communications officer. The man nodded and left. The Bishop was alone with the priest.

The Bishop sensed that the man felt called; he was no crackpot. "Let's pray," he told Thomas.

The Housekeeper
Witnesses

St. Catherine's housekeeper carried Fr. Thomas' mail in an empty cleaning bucket; the mail was steady.

The priest was gratified, holding out hope that he would be able to speak to the bishops.

Most Reverend Mario had not really told him no. At their meeting's close, he told him he would talk to the others, see what might be arranged. He warned that he was making no promises.

Maggie took the mail from the pail and set down her cleaning supplies. She told him that the Monsignor wanted her to deep clean the apartment. The head pastor wanted to show it to the Vicar.

"They're throwing me out," Fr. Thomas said, while looking over the letters that had come from many zip codes.

"You can stay here while I clean," Maggie said. "I'm washing floors, appliances, and windows. The Monsignor gave me a chore list."

"The Vicar has his own place now. It really seems like Monsignor Philip wants me to go soon," Fr. Thomas said.

"The only thing he said to me was that he didn't like all the cameras. Maybe you need to lie low," Maggie laughed.

Maggie held a broom and a dust pan, sweeping in the dirt.

"Did you notice the walker in the corner?" the priest said. "Maggie, I can walk on my own."

Maggie turned to look at "the metal legs." "I've heard you're telling people that you prayed to Clare Dall."

He took steps, as if he were marching in place. "Look at me," he said.

The housekeeper smiled. "I'm happy for you."

"Some people will say that you've lost your mind, you know? Monsignor Philip is telling folks that real miracles are very rare. He's telling people not to get excited, that your disability was probably not severe." Maggie went to the sink and filled her bucket with water. She took out a mop.

"The parish knows then?"

She slid a mop across the floor and back again: she mopped in rows. "There's a feeling that something big has happened; church members are just confused," she said.

Fr. Thomas chatted with the housekeeper and waited for her to finish her work. The priest was concerned that he had talked too much about his health. Clare and her lifelong commitment to the poor had to be his focus. Yet, he could hardly conceal his joy over his new strength. He would read mail.

The first batch of mail was an affirmation. People who were recipients of Dall's charity wrote to him. He suspected that some writers were older on account of their unsure handwriting. These folks knew Clare through the Urban Missions. They lived with her, volunteered services. Some writers liked her books, were inspired by her faith, her tendency to see God in all people. One woman recalled sharing a jail cell with Clare, who had been arrested at a Farm Workers protest.

Fr. Thomas drifted into a memory:

"Thank you, Tommy," Clare said. Tommy had freed his friend; he collected the bail money for her release. Clare was arrested at a protest of a distribution center: the protest was over low workers' wages. She had been locked up for three days, along the side of prostitutes and mostly petty criminals.

At first, she shared a cell with three other women; two women began calling each other names, so Clare was moved to solitary confinement as a safety precaution. She was given a Bible and told Tommy that she read the Gospel of John to pass the time.

"I came as soon as I could," Tommy said.

Tommy recalled the evening's heroic rescue efforts. The jail was housed in the municipal building, and he drove up and down the city streets; the combination of rain and colored lights distorted the roadways, making it hard to see. He finally found where Clare was being held.

Tommy went inside, could hear yelling, inmates carrying on. He told the lady at the desk that he wanted to bail out Clare Dall. The lady searched for Clare's release papers, stamped them, and told him to sit down. Clare came through a doorway to the lobby. She was undaunted.

"I want to become a Catholic," she told Tommy who was still thinking of the night's ordeal.

Tommy was driving on unfamiliar streets, was watching for signs. He heard

Simeon's Canticle

her but couldn't understand why jail and Catholicism went together.

Clare recited John 21:17

"He said to him a third time, 'Simon, son of John, do you love me?' Peter felt hurt because he had said the third time, 'Do you love me?' And he said to him, 'Lord, you know everything, you know that I love you.' Jesus said to him, 'Feed my sheep."

The passage had stuck in her mind after her incarceration. The Gospel of John led her to the Catholic Church.

Stir Fry Dinner

F r. Thomas neatly put the written treasures back in the envelopes. He would keep most of the responses. He noted that there was some criticism, mostly of him, of his anticipated role as a Catholic priest. Some wondered why he was not fighting abortion or working to deny gays' marriage.

He was expecting Fr. James: he was going to pick up groceries for a stir fry. Fr. Thomas believed that part of the joy of cooking was in the choice of wine. James entered the room, carrying two bags.

"One bag is full of letters," he said. "The Monsignor gave them to me to give to you. I don't think he's happy."

"Beef or chicken?" Fr. Thomas said. He removed the meat and vegetables from the paper bag.

"Beef," James announced. "You should be on friendly terms with the Monsignor. You have to live with him."

Fr. Thomas sipped some wine, waved his hand. "He's getting ready to put me out, wants the Vicar to live here." The older priest carried the bag of mail to the living room, set it next to his chair.

"You've started something. I think the Church now has to deal with its controversial champion of the poor."

Fr. Thomas agreed. He returned to the kitchen, began cutting broccoli florets, green peppers, onions.

"Are you keeping records of your conversations with people, especially the

Simeon's Canticle

press? You can get the best articles from newspapers' archives. You should create a folder for the Church, really preserve your story," Fr. James advised. Fr. Thomas appreciated his true interest and support.

He had not yet heard from Bishop Mario, but he felt certain that he would be given the chance to speak at the U.S. Bishops Conference.

He would have to prepare a speech, tell in a few well- chosen words why Clare Dall should be beatified, then canonized. Even while Fr. James moved around the kitchen, talking, chattering, he felt words entering into his mind. Was this how the Holy Spirit worked?

He had a guest who deserved his attention, who had kindly affirmed his changed fortune as far as health and accepted his spiritual explanation. Why couldn't he concentrate on the moment, the dinner, his good friend? The words kept coming into his thoughts. He couldn't seem to stop them.

Fr. James served dinner. While still slightly preoccupied, Fr. Thomas enjoyed the stir fry, having a second portion. He put the dirty plates in the dishwasher. He jiggled a nearly empty bottle of wine. The two priests wondered what would happen tomorrow; Clare Dall's cause was on their minds.

Fr. Thomas was up early. The traffic in front of St. Catherine's was like an alarm clock on some days. He looked out the window, wanting to see rush hour workers on the way to their jobs. He watched the bustle; hurried drivers switched lanes, he heard the honking car horns.

Closer to him, he saw a group coming his way. Monsignor Phillip was the man in the middle, to one side was the Vicar, to the other was Mike Gibbs.

Fr. Thomas greeted them at the door. The Monsignor explained that he came to show the apartment, and lead Mike Gibbs to the elderly priest's whereabouts.

"I hope you're making other housing arrangements," the Monsignor said.

He opened Fr. Thomas' bedroom door, the head pastor walked in. "There's a lot of furniture in this room. It's really quite large," Monsignor Philip said to the Vicar.

The Monsignor went into the kitchen, opened the refrigerator. "The appliances are new," he said.

Fr. Thomas stood back, watching, seeing the head pastor and his assistant causally go through his home.

Meanwhile Mike Gibbs looked the part of the outsider, standing alone in the foyer, waiting for Fr. Thomas' attention. The elderly priest went to him. "You want to talk to me," Fr. Thomas said.

"My committee notes that you've taken the Dall case to the media. You want to help your former friend very badly. We'll oppose any further consideration of Clare Dall's sainthood," Gibbs said.

"That doesn't surprise me," Fr. Thomas said. He looked at Gibbs and wondered why he had ever trusted him. His face looked unpleasant now, not friendly, or that of a man who wished him well.

Simeon's Canticle

The Monsignor and the Vicar stuck their heads into a small bathroom, turned back to Gibbs and Fr. Thomas.

"We'll be going now. Fr. Thomas, let me know your plans soon," he advised the priest. "Thank you," he said.

The two clergymen left

"The facts speak for themselves," Gibbs said, as he walked into the living room, turning to the priest. "Clare Dall's background, her mental illness, radical politics, and flawed character are highlighted in the committee's final report" He paused. "We are asking you to give up your ill-considered campaign, Fr. Thomas. We think you're too close to the Dall woman. You're not objective.

Fr. Thomas went to the door and opened it, as if to end the conversation and lead Mike Gibbs to the exit.

"Good-bye, Mr. Gibbs," he said.

The Maples

Fr. Thomas finished reading mail from the grocery sack. He had to find a place to live. That fact was a distraction. He thought about the home for retired priests. He wasn't feeling so old these days. He didn't know if he felt like playing Bible bingo. He imagined that the community made crafts.

He called his driver and asked him to take him to The Maples. Fr. Thomas thought he should see the place and not rely on his worried imagination or second-hand reports. Oddly, he wasn't so frightened of the community as he had been in the past. No matter where he lived, he was sure he wouldn't be weak or a ready burden. He thought he might even apply for a driver's license.

The church driver wasn't busy today and agreed to take him to the country, where The Maples was located. The driver remarked about the walker's absence; he observed the priest's certain steps.

There were wildflowers along the interstate. Fr. Thomas enjoyed the speedy hour-long ride to a low building with small rectangular windows. He wondered if the slender glass let in much light.

He entered what he thought was a community room. There were pictures of Jesus and the Holy Mother on the walls. There was a ping pong table and the television was on. Nobody was in sight.

He walked down the hall, seeing a few men eating at a cafeteria. He thought the

Simeon's Canticle

room smelled like hot dogs. Soda, juice dispensers lined the back wall. Doughnuts, bagels were displayed on racks.

He walked farther down the hall and saw the priests' bedrooms. Fr. Thomas smelled soaps, Lysol.

He saw a sign that marked the chapel. He peeked inside to see a large room; it had auditorium seating and looked more like a movie theater than a church. He saw the altar, the crucifix, and the tabernacle. Fr. Thomas bowed before the Eucharist and returned to the hallway. A few men passed him.

He stopped an attendant. "My name is Fr. Thomas Kelly, and I am thinking of moving here. Who should I talk to?"

"You'll have to talked to someone in the office, down the hall, on your right," he directed the priest.

The hallway was wide and its floor was a yellowing white linoleum. Fr. Thomas was keenly aware of a wheelchair outside the office's door.

The woman at the desk assured him that the retirement center had a room available. She told him to reserve it today if he was moving within the month. Fr. Thomas couldn't commit to the home.

The center's smell discouraged him; disinfectant, laundry detergent, boiled hot dogs. The many smells became an odor.

A priest was yelling, as if he were senile or in physical distress. Fr. Thomas just wanted to get back to St. Catherine's and his mail.

Simeon's Canticle

Monsignor Philip picked up his mail, handed to him, and stated that the letters were slowing down.

Fr. Thomas went to the head pastor's office as soon as he returned to the church, he needed to talk about moving; the Vicar already had a nice place, and he felt the move wasn't so necessary.

Modern religious prints decorated the Monsignor's office. Salvador Dali's "Sacrament of the Last Supper" was Philip's favorite; the framed print hung on the wall behind his desk.

The head priest had said Mass in the afternoon and changed into athletic clothing, shorts and a tee-shirt. He was going to run. The man was a runner and often participated in and organized charity races.

"The Vicar's residence should be in St. Catherine's rectory," the Monsignor told Fr. Thomas. "I want him closer to the church, easily available."

Fr. Thomas told of his visit to the retirement home. A room could be reserved, but he felt he was not ready for the community. His health had recently improved; he resisted changing his location.

"The plan is in motion," the Monsignor said. "Are you asking me to set the plan aside now? It cannot be done. I hate to be blunt, but you are a retired priest who doesn't contribute much to the parish." He put one foot up on a chair, so he could tie the strings on his shoe. "I'm sorry to say that."

"So, you put me in an old folks' home? I've put in my time at St. Catherine's. I really don't care to be treated as disposable. I'm advocating for Clare Dall, a Holy woman and a daughter of the Church.," Fr. Thomas said. "I'm in touch with the Bishop, and I like to continue my campaign for her."

"Thomas, how could I forget what you're doing, telling people that a former friend healed you? I don't suppose that you've seen a doctor. A doctor could probably explain your miracle. You created a circus here. No, I won't change plans for you now. You've forgotten your purpose," he said.

"I wish you understood," Fr. Thomas said, feeling like an old priest again. "I really wish you understood."

"Reserve that room, Thomas."

"There are only so many hours in the day, and I need to run," the Monsignor said. He walked to the door, expecting the older priest to follow.

Thomas did and was sad. He could not remember when he felt so sad.

He watched the man jog down the sidewalk in front of the sanctuary. Fr. Thomas went inside the church

A woman was seated in a pew near the altar. Otherwise, Fr. Thomas was alone in the large, sacred space. He sat in his usual spot, across from the stain glass picture of the fourth joyful mystery, The Presentation at the Temple. At the moment, joy seemed so impossible. He felt that he was being discarded like a worn winter sweater. He listened to the silence, focusing on sound.

The woman was softly saying, whispering the Rosary. Maybe, he should appeal to Mary, but he dismissed the idea of rote prayer. He needed to ask God in his own words for relief from how he felt. He said in

Simeon's Canticle

his interior voice: I'm an old man whom you have called. Help me, Father.

He heard the woman say the Rosary's closing litany. She stood, passed him on her way out. She smiled at him. He sat for a long while alone; the silence was complete. He'd go home now; he had to reserve his room at the retirement community. Monsignor Philip left him little choice.

The housekeeper left him a note, saying she changed his sheets. The apartment was clean, except for the opened and unopened mail. Fr. Thomas wanted to write to some people, the folks who knew Clare Dall at the more than 50 Urban Missions she had set up in cities across the country. The priest was surprised that he had connected with so many of Clare's friends.

The Bishop's News

He retrieved the Maples brochure; he needed the home's phone number. He picked up his phone; there was a missed call from the Diocese; there was a message; Bishop Mario said he had good news and wanted Thomas to return his call. Fr. Thomas immediately pressed the numbers.

Bishop Mario explained that the Conference director was following Thomas' story in the news, and he agreed to give the priest ten minutes before the bishops' lunch break. If the short time slot was acceptable, the man needed to know as soon as possible. "It's another miracle," the Bishop said.

Fr. Thomas had expected this call; he somehow knew that this was the next step, the next challenge. Bishop Mario gave him the organizer's contact information. The Bishop requested to preview the priest's speech draft two weeks before the meeting. Bishop Mario congratulated him.

When the priest said goodbye, his spirit had risen, lifted: he wasn't exactly happy. He felt as if he was meant to deliver a recommendation to the Conference. An incredible door had opened. He had a sense that events were happening as if they were fateful. He could only go along with them.

The next day, he called the Conference director and agreed to the limited time allotment, before lunch was fine. He also called the retirement community and held the empty room for one month. He would move in one month. He had much to do; he needed to work quickly.

News of Fr. Thomas' speaking bit travelled fast; Joey Cree sent out a press release, saying that a Diocese priest was on the national conference's agenda; the Church Bishops would consider a resolution to begin the process for Clare Dall's sainthood; it began with beatification; the voting results would be sent to the Vatican. The Pope, the Most Holy Father, was the final word. Fr. Thomas thought that the Church was leaning her way for a long while. His efforts were merely timely.

Fr. Thomas received congratulatory calls from priests in his own Diocese, and from clergyman around the country. Monsignor Philp called, saying he was delighted, he apologized for saying harsh words earlier.

Then there was Fr. James who became convinced of Clare Dall's holiness; he visited his now celebrated friend. He asked if Fr. Thomas would say Mass at his church next Sunday.

He began to study the Gospel of John. He was looking for inspiration about what he should tell the Conference. The Book seemed appropriate, because it led Clare to convert to Catholicism.

In John, Jesus said: "I give you a new commandment that you love one another. Just as I have loved you, you should love one another. By this everyone will know that you are my disciples.'

Fr. Thomas was convinced that love was behind Clare's lifelong actions. She joined the Catholic Church because it had the most potential, the power to transform God's love into an earthly reality. Clare thought the Mother Church was the right vehicle to carry His Will into just fruition.

The beliefs of her life were coming together; Fr. Thomas sat at his keyboard and composed a draft to present to Bishop Mario for approval. On his desk was a picture; it was taken on the day that he was ordained. He thought about his early life and years as a Catholic priest. Every effort, every action, every decision, culminated into his fortune today. He had witnessed the buds of holiness, he had a part in the formation of a person who might be considered by all a saint. He was satisfied; he could now go to the retirement community or wherever. He was at peace.

About the Author

Mattie McClane (Kristine A. Kaiser) is an American novelist, poet, and journalist. She is the second and youngest daughter born to James L. and Shirlie I. Myers in Moline, Illinois. Her father was a commercial artist and her mother worked as a secretary.

McClane's earliest education was in the Catholic schools. Her experience with their teachings deeply affected her. At a young age, she became aware of gender inequality. She credits her early religious instruction for making her think about "all kinds of truths" and ethical matters.

McClane's parents divorced when she was eight years old. Her mother remarried attorney John G. Ames and the new couple moved to a house beside the Rock River. The river centrally figures in McClane's creative imagination. She describes her childhood as being "extraordinarily free and close to nature."

McClane moved to Colorado and married John Kaiser in 1979, in Aurora, just East of Denver.

They then moved to Bettendorf, Iowa where they had three children. John worked as a chemist. Mattie became interested in politics, joining the local League of Women Voters. According to McClane, she spent her 20s "caring for young children and working for good government."

She graduated from Augustana College with a B.A. degree in the Humanities. She began writing a political column for Quad-Cities Online and Small Newspaper Group, based in Illinois.

Her family moved to Louisville, Kentucky where she continued with her journalism and then earned an M.A. in English from the University of Louisville. Critically acclaimed author Sena Jeter Naslund directed her first creative thesis, "Unbuttoning Light and Other Stories," which was later published in a collection.

She was accepted to the University of North Carolina at Wilmington's M.F.A. in Creative Writing Program, where she wrote the short novel Night Ship, working under the tutelage of Pulitzer Prize winning author Alison Lurie. McClane studied with Dennis Sampson in poetry also. She graduated in 1999.

She would write a column for the High Point Enterprise in North Carolina. She would later write for the News and Observer. McClane has regularly published commentary for over 25 years.

Mattie McClane is the author of *Night Ship: A Voyage of Discovery* (2003), *River Hymn: Essays Evangelical and Political* (2004), *Wen Wilson* (2009), *Unbuttoning Light: The Collected Short Stories of Mattie McClane* (2012), *Now Time*

(2013), *Stations of the Cross* (2016), and *The Mother Word: An Exploration of the Visual* (2017).

She lives in North Carolina.

9 780972 246682